Murder in Miami

TROUBLED GIRLS FIND LOVE

KATHRYN REIGN

KATHRYN REIGN PUBLISHING

Copyright

Murder in Miami

© Copyright 2023 Kathryn Reign

Cover Design by Les (germancreative)

Murder in Miami

Murder in Miami Blurb

Who would've ever thought that a small-town girl from West Virginia would end up in prison?

Certainly not me.

And certainly not Dawson, the brooding bad boy who stole my virginity.

But not my heart.

No, that belongs to someone other than the man I'm supposed to be faithful to.

Ross. The new kid in school.

He's perfect for me in every way, but he's **not** my boyfriend.

And I can't choose!

One thing leads to another, and my entire life changes forever.

Contents

Chapter One

"Amber, please! Don't do this! I beg you; don't do this!"

"Shut up! Shut up!" His voice sounded like nails down a chalkboard inside my ears, and if I'd had my second cup of coffee this morning, I may have just been a little more lenient. But I'm tired. I'm so tired of all the games, of all the lies, of the fucking ultimatum. "Just shut up, and let me think!"

I didn't plan for this to happen. Hell, I didn't even think I'd show up. Throwing on my pajamas and climbing into bed was my way of saying "no way in hell." I thought that if I slept through the night, I'd wake up the next morning scar-free.

But instead, somehow, I found my way here, holding a gun in my hand and aiming it at the man I once loved.

"Please, Amber. I'm sorry. For everything! You don't have to do this." His voice continued to stab against my brain, and every word felt like someone was ripping off a fucking nerve.

"I don't have to do this? I don't have to do this?! The nerve of you even saying that after what you've put me through, and now you have the audacity to ask me to stop?" I found myself yelling at him, my voice growing louder and louder by the second.

To be honest, I didn't even know why I'd been so angry. And if you asked, I couldn't pinpoint the exact moment when the words that came out of his mouth turned into a bullet straight through his head. But it did.

And as I found myself trying to vigorously shake the anguish and stabbing pain out from my brain, I also found myself staring into my former lover's eyes, blood dripping from his mouth, followed by his body collapsing onto the ground and the shrieking scream of a female's voice.

Wait? Who else was here? I thought we were the only ones. Then who the fuck was yelling like a banshee that had just taken a knife to the heart?

Oh, right. Now I remember. It's my voice. I was the one screaming like a banshee.

"I killed him," I whisper to the two older men standing in front of me, tears dripping onto the handcuffs that tightly wrap around my wrists. "I killed him!"

The metal bars slam shut as they thrust me inside a cold, dark cell, with nothing but a narrow bed and what resembled half a toilet bowl keeping me company. I turn around, screaming after the men as they begin to walk away.

"Wait! I... I can't stay here! I have to see him. I have to tell him I'm sorry!" I wrap my fingers around the metal bars, gripping with all the strength I could possibly muster, shaking it back and forth and screaming for the two men to come back.

"Should've thought of that before you shot him," one of them yells back from a distance, the echo bouncing off the walls.

Shot him. Yeah, I did that alright.

JUNIOR YEAR WAS SUPPOSED to be the greatest year of my high school career… at least, that's what my parents told me when we moved all the way to Miami from our little town of Green Bank.

"You'll make friends!" she said.

"You'll have fun," he said.

She said, he said. They're all a bunch of lies.

Let me tell you this. When a parent tells you that you're the image of perfection, that you'll go far in life, that you'll never fail, they're full of shit. This fairytale world didn't exist in my little bubble of hell called "junior year." Otherwise, I wouldn't be shriveled up in nothing but my gym shorts and a granny's bra, shielding myself from the bucket full of trash that was being hurled at me from a hundred feet away.

"What's wrong, loser?" That's Cindy, head of the cheerleading team. She had locks smooth as silk and glossy as gold, the complete opposite of my tangled mess of greasy, split ends, and now, wads of gum. "You want your mommy?" She burst out into laughter along with her little posse beside her, her perky tits flopping up into the air, and her flawless face without even a single wrinkle as she continued enjoying her amusement at my demise.

To this day, I still don't know why she decided to target me like that. I wasn't special or different. I didn't get better grades than her, and I certainly wasn't more attractive than her. It was like she's Cinderella, and I'm the ugly stepsister—always the bridesmaid, never the bride.

I was a nobody, and she had everything. A rich dad, a sports car, the hottest guy in school with a smoldering look that could make anybody wet.

Why me?

"That's enough, ladies! That's enough!" That's Karen Burgundy, the gym teacher.

Everyone calls her by her first name because she'd told us that it made her seem bitchier, and no one wants to mess with a bitch. She's a widow… five times, to be exact. And she'd always tell us that her exes are no longer here because they didn't listen to her. We all thought she was just joking at first, but then it became obvious that something was just off about her. Even so, no one dared to ever investigate. They didn't want to become victim number six.

"Oh, Karen," Cindy spoke back. "We're just having a little fun! Aren't we, Amber?" She looked over at me, a look on her face that said nothing but, "I'm gonna kill you if you don't follow along."

I shivered, not from the cold air rushing through the open window that was now blowing onto my half-naked body, but from the genuine fear of what that girl is capable of doing to me.

"I… I…" She glares at me again. This time, discreetly tossing the tampon applicator she had in her hand over at me without Karen noticing. "I… Yeah, we're just having fun."

"Cindy! Into my office. Now!" Apparently, she *had* noticed.

"What the hell? She said she's having fun!" Cindy retorted, crossing her arms over chest and tucking them under her breasts.

"I said, now!" Karen wasn't having it, and as terrifying as I thought Cindy was, she was nothing compared to the angry wrath of Karen Burgundy.

"Ugh, fine! I bet all your exes killed themselves, just so they could get away from you."

A series of oohs and ahs sounded in the locker room as Karen marched over toward Cindy, snatched her wrist, and pulled her out the door. The other girls all whipped out their phones to record the whole fiasco, but it wasn't like this was anything new. Cindy was always mouthing off to the teachers.

But if anyone could. It's her. Not everyone's father can contribute billions of dollars to their kid's school.

I reached up to grab the window sill above my head once everyone had left, struggling to pull myself up from off the ground. My knees were bruised from when they'd kicked me, throwing on the sandals made from stone they all had stored in the locker before wailing against my legs. I assumed they were made from stone. Certainly felt like it.

When I finally made my way over to my own locker and opened it, I was so unsurprised that I wasn't even mad. Of course, they'd taken all my clothes. Of course, I'd have to now walk around in shorts that looked like my grandma's knickers and a bra that's meant for a maiden in the eighteen hundreds.

Just my luck. Junior year is really shaping up, Mom, just like you said.

I hugged my books against my chest as I made my way down the hall and out to the bus stop. Thank fuck that phys ed was my last class of the day. I definitely didn't want to linger around here any longer than I had to, especially almost nude.

A hundred feet remaining to the double doors. Eighty feet. Fifty feet left. Almost there.

"Hey, Amber!" Shit, that voice. The very voice that continues to haunt my dreams every night.

I turned around, and there was Cindy, dressed in her cheerleading uniform and surrounded by both the cheerleading and football teams. She certainly was the head honcho, but it makes me think if she'd end up just like me without all her loyal fans.

"You fucking got me detention for a week! A week! AND my dad canceled my party this weekend." The crowd around her booed as she continued. "You better watch your back, you little cunt. One way or another, I'll get my revenge." Then she pulled out a pair of scissors from her little Hello Kitty backpack and snipped the straps off my bra.

"What the hell did you do that for?!" I shrieked as I hurried to gather myself from being exposed to the entire school. Everyone just stood there, laughing at me, and in that moment, I felt so vulnerable with my bare back exposed for everyone to see.

"Snitches get stitches," was all Cindy could say before taking out her phone and pressing record.

"I didn't snitch on you! You were just too stupid to fool her!" I was shouting, but I didn't know why. I didn't want payback against her; I just wanted to run home, lock myself in the closet, and never come out again.

"Well," Cindy chuckled, "at least I'm not the one in my underwear."

"What?"

And less than a second later, I found my gym shorts being torn in half and falling onto the ground. Laundry day wasn't until later that night, and I'd been ashamed even at home to wear my purple and green polka dot granny panties. Now I found myself sporting them like I was a model prancing down the runway.

"Hey, everyone, look! Amber the Snitch here wears her mom's underwear! So embarrassing!" Then Cindy leaned in closer. "Maybe if you'd spend less time snitching and more time at the mall, you wouldn't be such an outcast!"

I wanted to yell back, scream at her even, spit in her face. But I knew I had been defeated. Anything else I threw her way would only act as ammo against me, and simply leaving was the best thing I could do for myself.

I forced myself to hold back my tears as I clutched the books closer to me and ran out the doors. Screw the bus stop. I didn't live that far from school. I'd have better luck not being seen just running home instead. Undergarments and sneakers weren't exactly the trendiest look, but if Regina George can pull of such hideous fashion, why couldn't I?

I was less than two blocks from home when I collided into something, or someone, who would eventually change my life forever.

Chapter Two

"Whoa, easy there—" The man who ran into me stopped mid-speech and looked me up and down, his face quickly turning a bright shade of pink. "You're... You're—"

"I know!" I shouted, bending over to gather my belongings and quickly covering my bare chest back up.

"But... why? You work in a strip club or something? A little young, but I suppose—"

I peered at him closer as he spoke. He was definitely trying too hard to pull off that bad boy look. I mean, a leather jacket AND spikes? Not to mention the very unflattering half-lit cigarette that was dangling from in between his lips. Sure, I despised the cheerleaders and the jocks, but his type was right up there also on my list of losers to stay away from.

"Are you serious?" I cut him off. "What kind of stripper carries around a thick ass textbook on Trigonometry?"

"One who's trying not to completely disappoint her father?" he teased, batting an eye at me.

I cringed, but let my guard down. Then I remembered that I was no longer covering myself up, and I was completely flashing this stranger standing in front of me. I quickly raced my arms back up, crossing them over my chest. "I have to go."

"Wait!" He called out to me and grabbed onto one of my arms, catching me off-guard and causing me to drop my books and expose my bare breasts to this strange man once again.

"What the fuck, dude?" I yelled out to him. "Why can't you just leave me alone?"

"I'm... I'm sorry. I didn't mean to do that. I just wanted to know your name."

"Why?" My face was growing hot with fury, but my heart was also beginning to warm up. For a bad boy, he looked pretty cute when he's all ashamed and timid.

"Because I think you're really pretty." His eyes traveled down to the lower half of my body, and as I caught him staring straight at green and purple polka dots, he said, "Even if you *are* sporting a Barney-inspired look."

"If you're just gonna insult me, I may as well just be on my way. Is that the only reason you stopped me?"

"What? No, I never got a chance to introduce myself. I'm Dawson, by the way." He extended his hand out, but I refused to do the same.

"Amber," I answered him, "and I'd shake your hand, under different circumstances."

"Oh, right. My bad." He withdrew his hand back and ran a few fingers through his hair. "It's nice to meet you, Amber. Such a pretty name. Here, take my jacket. It'll cover you up a bit more." As I watched him take the leather jacket off his back, I couldn't help but stare at those delicious biceps that he'd been hiding beneath it.

I grabbed the jacket from him, temporarily placing my textbooks down on the ground and showing my boobs to the whole town, Dawson included, so I could throw it over my shoulders. Luckily, it was long enough to cover even my polka dot butt, and I no longer needed to use Trigonometry as my own personal wardrobe.

"Thanks, you have no idea the day I've had." I thanked him, finally extending my hand for a handshake. "You're literally a lifesaver."

"Ha-ha, I can imagine. It's not every day I see a girl running around in her underwear." Then he winked. "Not that I'm complaining."

"My house is only a couple blocks away. If you wanna walk with me, I can give you your jacket back after I put on something decent." I gestured over to my right, waiting for him to accept the invitation and follow me.

"Nah," he simply said.

"Nah...? Do you want it back now? But I just—"

He laughed again. "Of course not, silly! I meant 'nah' as in, if I take it back now, how else am I going to see you again?"

Clever. I like it, but a bit odd. I've never been someone to attract men. Sure, I'd been pretty back in Green Bank, but with a population of under two hundred and most of the girls there dressed in hay and manure, I didn't have much competition. But here? These Miami supermodels make me look like one of them had just crapped me out after a good night at Taco Bell.

"You mean a date?" I asked him.

I'm not stupid. I knew that's what he was reaching for, but I was loving the attention, and the more flattery I could get from someone, the better.

"No, I mean I wanna get you all alone in a warehouse so I could put a bullet through your head. Of course, I mean a date!"

That was oddly specific. I wondered if this meeting was even accidental. Maybe he'd been roaming the streets of Miami for weeks, scouting out unsuspecting girls whom he could kidnap and take back to his little dungeon to murder. Maybe I was walking into my own death.

I had half a mind to turn around and run away, taking his jacket with me and putting in a restraining order for the sake of my own life, but then I looked into his eyes, and fuck, I'm such a sucker for those puppy-dog eyes. So, I gave in.

"Fine." I sighed. "Where're we going?"

"Tomorrow night at six. We'll meet again here. It'll be our special spot." Then he winked at me and walked away.

I sighed, wrapping the jacket around me so it snugged around my thin frame. I didn't even notice myself blushing until the heat started emanating from my face. Dawson. Miami might not be so bad after all.

THE NEXT EVENING, I made sure to show up properly dressed, though I'm sure I would've become his favorite woman if I hadn't. I didn't have much—moving from such a small town where my parents didn't have much, and the girls I hung around cared more about their studies than a competition of who's the sexiest in town.

But Miami was humid! And I knew I needed to sport something other than sweatpants and a shaggy sweater. So, I pulled out an old pair of jeans, and with my trusty pair of scissors, I turned it into frayed shorts. I then threw a baggy t-shirt over the top half of my body and tied a knot on the back so it looked more fitting.

"Wow, I didn't expect to see you with so much clothes on," Dawson teased when I met him at the spot. Honestly, even a minute of standing there began to bring back horrific memories of the day before, but the sun had set, and being so new to the city, luckily not very many people would recognize me.

"I could say the same about you." I grinned, looking up and down his all-leather look. "Do you own anything else other than leather?"

He winked. "I got a few pairs of boxers. Wanna see?"

I shook my head. "I'm good."

"Ha! Good, cause I ain't wearing any."

"Do you always joke around like that?" I asked him, rolling my eyes at his poor sense of humor.

"Who's joking? I actually like going commando every once in a while. It's actually very freeing. You should try it some time." He raised a brow at me. "You know, what you were doing yesterday, but the... opposite?"

"Very funny. Not!" I crossed my arms over my chest. "Is that why you asked me to come out here tonight? So you could humiliate me even more than I've already been?" Then I threw my hands up in the air. "God! I knew my family should've never moved here. Miami is full of nothing but a shitty bunch of—"

And before I could even register what was happening, Dawson was kissing me. He'd grabbed me by the shoulders, spun me around, and planted his full lips against mine, massaging both my lips and tongue like he was kneading a roll of dough with his mouth.

Kissing strangers weren't my thing. Never have been. But when someone as hot as Dawson, with lips made of magic, starts kissing you, you'd be a fool to not kiss back. So warm. So inviting. Like we've been doing this for years, and this kiss signified the start of the rest of our lives together.

"So, what were you saying?" he asked with a grin when we pulled away. "Miami is full of nothing but a shitty bunch of...?"

"I... I... I don't remember."

"That's what I thought." Then he leaned in and kissed me again.

Chapter Three

I'd been dating Dawson for a little short of six months now, and my reputation in school had skyrocketed to superstar levels. I went from being the loser, new girl running around in her underwear to the most popular girl in school, with her hot arm candy by her side. Even Cindy and her gang of plastic dolls started to treat me like I was someone famous! Inviting me to sit with them at lunch and even go shopping with them after school at the mall.

I didn't know who I was anymore, but I wasn't sure if I liked who I was becoming. I'd never been one to have so much popularity around me, and my roots of growing up as a small-town girl were beginning to fade.

I liked Dawson. I really did. And there's a ninety percent chance that I'm not just saying that because he took my virginity.

Yeah, I said it. About a week after our first kiss, I gave in. We weren't even officially dating yet, and that had only been my second time seeing him. But he said all the right things. Told me the words that every teenage girl wanted to hear.

I love you.

He said it! Not me. Well, not at first.

But then I found myself sitting in his car, his hand sliding up my skirt as he kissed me first on my lips, and then slowly down my neck, and the next thing I knew, he was leaning the passenger seat of the car back and climbing on top of me.

"I want you, Amber," he whispered into my ear, sliding his hand further and further up until I felt chills course through my body.

I didn't stop him. In fact, I wasn't even completely sure what to do in that moment. He was the first boy I'd ever been with, and I had no concept of what "moving too fast" meant. So, I just tilted my head back and closed my eyes, letting both his hands and tongue roam around my body—his mouth encircling my breasts, and his bare hips swaying against mine—and when I felt something hard and warm enter inside of me, I gasped.

"It's okay. I'll take good care of you. I promise." Then he kissed me again, thrusting himself faster and faster, deeper and deeper, until a loud sound escaped from his lips, and he collapsed on top of me.

"I love you," he whispered into my ear.

"I love you, too."

And now, I was beginning to second guess whether I had actually meant what I'd said, or whether the first orgasm I'd ever experienced sent me so far over the edge that I was even willing to say those same three words to a pigeon waddling down the street.

"Hey, babe. I'll catch you after school. Gotta go take care of some things." Dawson pulled me out of my thoughts and gave me a kiss on the cheek.

I flashed him a light smile as he started walking off with a few of his buddies, barely even registering my response. It didn't seem like he really cared, anyway. Hell, I didn't really care. Dawson was way out of my league, and whether he's with me for me or as arm candy, I'll never really know.

However, as I turned back around, a glaring light blinded my eyes, and it took me a second before I noticed the face in it. A boy, brown hair, and glasses that seemed just a little too large for his face. But he reminded me of the boys I used to know back in Green Bank, the down-to-earth homebodies that I'd grown up with.

And he was new. Well, at least to me, he was. But to me, half the school was still new. Despite everyone knowing me, I'd become enclosed in my little circle I liked to call "Dawson and I."

"Hey, four eyes! Watch where you're going!" I heard behind me as I turned back to my locker to grab my books for next period.

When I turned to face the boy again, I saw Dawson and his buddies knocking into him, pushing him around before eventually kicking him to the ground and walking away laughing. I liked Dawson, but he could be a real ass sometimes. However, I guess it was good to have someone like him on my side. Otherwise, I'd probably be scrambling around the ground for my things also.

But my heart felt for him. It felt like it was just yesterday when I found myself crouched down inside the locker room, bombarded by Cindy and her gang. It's never easy being the new kid. The least I could do was help him.

I walked over and picked up a book, Introduction to Electromagnetism. "Here, I think this belongs to you." I crouched down and handed it over to him.

A timid look glared up at me, and I could see the thin blue ring around his dark brown eyes. How unique.

"Yeah, thanks." He gave me a weak smile and gathered the rest of his things before standing back up. I followed, the textbook still in my hands.

"Electromagnetism, huh? Sounds difficult. You must be really smart."

But he just raised his brows at me and grabbed the book from me when I extended my hand. "Come on, we both know that's not the reason you came over here. To tell me that I'm smart."

He really is smart. "You're right. I saw how those guys treated you, and I just wanted to apologize on their behalf. I know what it's like being the new kid. I thought I'd help you out a little."

"I don't need anyone's pity. And why are you apologizing for them? You know them or something?"

My face turned red. "I... I... no. I don't. I just know they're a bunch of bullies, and you didn't deserve that."

"Thanks. Name's Ross, by the way." He extended his hand out to me.

"Amber."

"Is today your first day also, Amber?

I shook my head. "I've actually been here for about six months now. Still getting the hang of things, though. I'm originally from Green Bank—"

"West Virginia?"

I nodded.

"No way! I'm from Dunmore! I just moved here last week!"

"Wow," I chuckled, "and here I was thinking I'm the odd one out."

"I guess we can now *both* be weirdos together." He chuckled back. Suddenly, the bell rang. He turned to me and waved. "Well, gotta get over to, you know," he pointed at his textbook and then behind him, "this and all. Gotta keep up the grades. You know how it is."

"Yeah, uh, sure." I didn't, not really. I'd never been into

school or getting straight As, but he was definitely the type to care.

"Hey, this might be a little too forward, but would you be interested in grabbing some ice cream with me after school? I don't know much about this chaos of a city, and it'd be great to have a fellow West Virginian show me around."

I paused. I'd promised Dawson I'd meet up with him at the arcade after school. Him and his buddies were going to attempt to beat a new game that had just released, and he needed me there for emotional support.

But I'd also just made a friend, someone I could actually connect with. Did I really want to give that up for a game?

"Sure." I smiled at Ross. "I'd love to."

"Great! See you in about...," he looked down at his watch, "two hours and thirty-six minutes! It's a date!"

I pushed my way out through the double doors of the front entrance and could barely catch my breath. What the hell was I doing? Did he really just say *date*? Ugh! I mean, he's cute and all, for a shy guy, but I'm with Dawson. Was I really just about to bail on him for another dude?

Suddenly, my phone rang, and I jumped up with a mini heart attack.

"Hello?" I answered.

"Hey, babe! We still on for later? I can't wait to have my lucky charm with me as I crush this!" It was Dawson.

"Hey, don't hate me, but I was wondering if I could skip. I think I ate something bad during lunch, and now I'm not feeling too great. I think I might just go home and go straight to bed."

"Shucks, well, that blows. I was really counting on you to be there!"

"I'm sorry, babe. Next time, I promise to be there for you. I'll even wear a mini skirt and carry pom poms."

"I'd take you in a mini skirt any day, sweet cheeks. And I

don't mean your face." I didn't need to see it. He was clearly giving me his signature wink. "How about I come over after and see how you're feeling? Maybe cheer you up?"

"I'd like that. But just remember to come over after seven. That's when my mom leaves for work."

"Aw, she doesn't wanna stay for the fun?"

"Dawson!"

"I'm just messin' with you. Seven it is. I love you, babe."

"I love you, Dawson." And as I hung up, I twitched my face. I'd been saying "I love you" to him for months, but it never seemed to get any easier the more I did it.

Chapter Four

I met up with Ross at Kazoo's. It's a little further away from the city than I would've liked, but I couldn't risk Dawson finding out that I'd ditched him for another guy. Turned out, we both liked pistachio ice cream drizzled with a hefty serving of caramel sauce. I could've sworn to my grave that I was the only one who liked that combination.

"So, tell me, Amber, why'd you move to Miami? I mean, it's so different from Green Bank!" Ross mumbled in between spoonfuls to his mouth.

I shrugged. "My parents just wanted a change, I guess. My dad got a job offer that he said he couldn't turn down, but I know he'd been eyeing Miami for quite some time now, and this was just the perfect excuse to make that jump."

"But... but you don't fit in!"

"What the hell is that supposed to mean? I fit in just fine!"

"Amber, look around you."

I quickly glanced around. All the girls walking around outside were dressed like they had just come from the beach, and all the guys looked like they forgot to do this week's laundry. I guess Ross was right. I didn't exactly fit in with my purple cardigan.

Then I shook my head. "What's with the interrogation, anyway? I could ask you the same thing! It's not like you belong here anymore than I do!"

"That's the point. I don't! That's why I was so ecstatic when I found out that you're just like me. I was about ready to hop on the next bus out of town before I met you today." Ross shot me a bashful grin, a grin that said, "I know I'm not the best grape in the bunch, but please be nice to me."

And I couldn't help but release a light giggle. He wasn't Dawson, confident and brooding, but Ross was sweet, and I could really see us becoming great friends.

HOURS WENT BY, and I didn't notice how late it was getting outside until Kazoo's started smelling like detergent.

"Ah, shit! What time is it?" I glanced down at my watch. Just ten minutes before seven. Fuck. "I... I have to go." I quickly stuttered to Ross and grabbed my things, throwing down a ten-dollar bill for my ice cream before running toward the door.

"Wait!" he shouted after me. I stopped. I shouldn't have, but I did. "When can we hang out again? I had such a great time with you."

I felt my face blush. It wasn't something I thought I'd ever do with someone other than Dawson, but the way Ross looked at me just made me feel things inside. "I'm not sure. Soon?" I hesitated. "I think I might be busy for a while."

"Let me at least give you my number, in case you change your mind." I barely had a chance to stop him before he jotted his number down on a piece of napkin and tucked it into the side pocket of my backpack. Then he gave me a pat on the shoulder. "If I get the honor of hanging out with you again, then that'd be superb. If not, then I guess I'll just be that pathetic loser at school who longs after you like a puppy dog."

"That's a terrible joke." I chuckled and pushed open the door. "I'll see you around, Ross."

"See you around."

I made it back home with just enough time to throw myself into my robe and quickly shuffle up my hair. I needed to be just convincing enough so that Dawson would think I was home all night. I hated lying to him, and it wasn't even like I was doing anything wrong. But Dawson and Ross clearly didn't get along, and I bet just the mention of his name would set my boyfriend off.

A second after I washed my makeup off my face, the bell rang. I steadied myself and made my way downstairs, where I saw Dawson peering through the front window.

"Hey, babe. How're you feeling?" He handed me a bouquet of flowers when I flung the door open. "Oh! And I got you some chicken noodle. It's not homemade, but the host at the diner said it's still pretty tasty."

Fuck. Of course, he turns into the best boyfriend ever on the day I decide to betray him.

"Thanks," I gave him a soft smile, "this is all very sweet of you. You didn't have to do all this."

"Why wouldn't I? You're my girl. And I take care of my girl. So, how you feeling? Well enough to kiss?" Dawson closed the door behind him as he walked inside the house, and he drew me into a bear hug before rubbing my shoulders. "I missed you this afternoon. I crushed the game, but I definitely could've gotten a better score." He leaned in and kissed me on the cheek. "It's because I was missing my lucky charm."

"I'll be there next time, I promise. I'll make it up to you."

Then he winked at me. "Or you can just make it up to me now." And before I knew it, he scooped me up by the legs and carried me up to my room, where he lightly threw my body against the bed and hovered his own body over me, planting kisses across my neck and beginning to untie the robe.

"Dawson, wait. I'm sick, remember?" I put a hand to his chest and stopped him. But if there was one thing I knew well about Dawson, was that he didn't let anything—and I mean anything—get in the way between him and a warm, slimy hole.

"Babe, I'd rather risk getting sick than spend another day without your body pressed up against mine." Then he leaned back down and continued with the kisses.

His lips felt so warm, so dominating, that it brought me back to when we first made love, when he took my virginity. And I felt myself giving in instantly, almost forgetting where I'd really been and the reason why he was even here tonight.

I whispered a moan as he pulled his shirt over his head and came back down, reaching a hand off to one side of the bed as I nibbled on his left ear, his favorite spot. Then I heard a crinkle when he extended his reach, and memories of why that crinkle existed shot back into my thoughts.

"What's this?" He reached into the netted side pocket of my backpack and pulled out *the* crinkled sheet. And when he unfolded it, my heart dropped. "Who the *fuck* is Ross?" His bellow almost shot through my ceiling with how loud it sounded, and he climbed off the bed to throw his shirt back on.

"What? No one!" I fumbled to come up with a decent enough lie. "Just a friend from school."

"Amber, come on. I know who your friends are, and you definitely don't know someone named Ross. Besides, what kind of friend draws a heart next to their number?"

"Umm, a cheeky one?"

"Amber! Are you fucking cheating on me?"

"No!" I jumped off the bed and grabbed him by the

hands, squeezing them tight in hopes that it'd quell his anger enough for me to explain myself.

"Then explain this!"

"He's just a friend! I swear! He moved here from my state, and we just got to talking. But we didn't do anything! We just went out for ice cream." God, I wish I could take back my words sometimes.

"Today? Is that why you ditched me? To hang out with some other guy? Were you even sick?" I bowed my head and slowly shook it. "You're unbelievable, Amber! I give you nothing but love, and you go behind my back with some other dude?"

"Well, you never even asked if I wanted to spend my day at the arcade."

"That doesn't give you an excuse to cheat on me!"

"I wasn't—" He was gone before I could say anything else, slamming his way out of my bedroom, down the stairs, and out the front door.

Chapter Five

It'd been three days since our fight, and Dawson refused to pick up any of my calls. Even when I'd see him at school and call out his name, he'd just run in the opposite direction, forever giving me the cold shoulder.

"Give him time," one of his buddies told me once. "He just needs some time to think. He loves you. He'll come around."

And I would've believed him had it not been for Cindy and her fat mouth.

"You look particularly happy today. Something happen?" I overheard Megan, one of Cindy's clones, on the third day asking her by the lockers. I backed up an inch and hid behind the water fountain. Nearly half the school knew about Dawson and my fight, and I couldn't deal with any more drama than I already was.

"Well, Meg, generally, I don't kiss and tell, but if you must know. I had sex." Cindy sung.

"I don't get it. You and Jordan have sex all the time. Isn't it like... your thing?"

"Ah, but that's the best part." She leaned in closer to her

friend, but I could still hear every word. "It wasn't with Jordan."

"You cheated—?"

"Shh, tell the whole school, will ya?"

"Then who?"

Cindy smirked. "Dawson."

I felt my heart immediately drop down to my stomach as I stood there frozen, listening to Cindy describe every detail—from the way he encircled her fake breasts with his tongue, to the way he played with her until she couldn't contain herself anymore, to the way he inserted himself into her bare body as if they were two pieces of a jigsaw puzzle.

So, that's why he didn't answer my calls? Because he was fucking Cindy?

I couldn't breathe, and I definitely couldn't stand there for another second listening to Cindy tell the whole school how big my boyfriend's dick was. I had to get out of here. I had to go. I had to—

I spun myself around and bolted for the double doors. I could feel my whole world around me suffocating me, and I didn't know how much longer I could contain myself before passing out onto the ground. And I didn't stop until I made my way out into the school parking lot and collapsed into myself. My stupid parents should've never left Green Bank. I was just fine where I was in my cushy lifestyle.

"Amber?"

I spun my head toward the voice and saw none other than Ross himself walking toward me. Tears were still heavily flowing down my cheeks, and I quickly rushed to wipe them away before he could realize that I'd been crying.

"Ross," I managed to choke out, "wh-what are you doing here?"

"I saw you run out while heading to bio and wanted to

check in on you. You okay?" Then he peered closer at me. "Looks like you'd been crying."

Damn. He noticed.

"I-I'm fine. Just allergies."

Ross shook his head. "I get allergies like crazy, and I can spot one from a mile away. This isn't it. Besides, if you don't tell me, I can always easily find out myself. I'm a genius, remember?"

I drew a slight grin from his joke, then I sighed. Time to spill the tea.

"It's Dawson. You know, the one who bullied you? He's actually my boyfriend." I cringed, expecting to see a look of surprise on his face at the shocking news. Instead, he just shrugged, like he'd already known. "Anyway, we got into a huge fight, and he's been ignoring me for a few days now. And I just found out that he'd been sleeping with Cindy, my sworn enemy, and now it just feels like my world is falling apart."

I started sniffling again, and felt a wave of comfort wash over me when Ross pulled me in for a hug. "Don't beat yourself up over it too much. That guy's kinda an asshole, anyway. You deserve someone better."

"Why's that?"

"Huh?"

"Why's he an asshole?" I repeated.

"Well, first, he's a bully. All I ever see him do at school is get high in the boy's restroom, and you might not have noticed, but I've seen the way he treats you compared to how he treats other girls. It's almost like he's just with you because you put out."

"You've known about us?"

He shrugged. "Not that hard to put the pieces together when you two are literally the only thing anyone can talk about these days."

Why was he being so nice to me? Even after I'd lied to

him? I dropped my head down onto his shoulder when he pulled away slightly. "I'm sorry for not telling you. I didn't think you'd be my friend if I told you I was dating the guy who beat the crap out of you."

"Nah, it's cool. His actions don't define who you are. Besides, if I lost you, who else would I talk about the Mountaineers with?"

"We don't even like football!" I exclaimed and gave him a playful push.

"Heh, yeah, but I like knowing I have the option. Come on, let's go back inside. Get through this last period, and we can go watch a movie or something. Take your mind off of all this." He extended his hand out for me to take.

I nodded, grabbed his soft, baby skin hand, and together, we walked back inside... just to find Cindy's half-naked body pressed up against Dawson against the lockers, and her kissing him hard on the lips. "Jordan was never man enough for me. I'm glad I dumped his ass for you, sexy, sexy, Dawson."

"L-Let's get o-out of h-here," I stuttered and pulled Ross back toward the doors with me.

"But school isn't over yet—"

"I don't care!" I shouted, but everyone was too busy fawning over Cindy and Dawson to care.

I dropped Ross' hand, ran through the parking lot, and down the closest street. I needed to get as far away from here as possible. I needed to get away from Dawson, from Cindy, from this whole fucking city! I hated it here!

Chapter Six

I ran and ran until my legs started to feel like jelly. I stopped and leaned against a fence, catching my breath. *I should just hop on the next bus back to West Virginia and leave all this behind. My parents can stay if they want to, but no way in hell am I gonna.*

"Jesus, Amber! You're fast!" Ross panted next to me seconds later.

"You followed me?"

"Of course! I care about you. I saw what happened back there, and if I were in your shoes, I'd have done the same. I just wanted to make sure you didn't jump off a bridge or something."

I rolled my eyes. "I'm upset, not suicidal."

"Yeah, but still."

"What about last period?"

"Making sure you're okay is more important. I already have enough credits to get into college. School is just a hobby to me now."

"You really are smart, aren't you?" I asked. When he didn't respond, I followed up with, "How about that movie then?"

"I guess? Now that we're both out. But theaters won't let us in there until after three. You know, to prevent people from sneaking out of school early? Like us?"

But I shook my head. "Let's just go back to my place. My mom's working double shifts today. She won't be home for a while."

"Are you sure? I don't wanna feel like I'm intruding or anything."

"Positive."

When we got back to my house, I threw my shoes against the staircase and popped into the fridge to grab a couple beers. Dad always had way more lying around than he needed. He'd never notice a few missing here and there.

"Here," I said to Ross as I handed him one.

"Beer? Amber, we're underage!"

"So? It's not like adults are that responsible either when they drink." Truth be told, I only had my first drink after I met Dawson. He handed me a cold one after we'd made out in his car and told me it'd make me feel a lot better. I nearly threw up after my first sip, but after a while, my body started feeling looser, and it felt good to be free from my worries for even just a few minutes.

But still, he continued shaking his head, like a real party pooper.

"Humor me, would you?" I insisted and extended the bottle closer to him.

"Amber, I can't." His voice was low, like something I'd said bothered him.

"Why are you being so pathetic?" I nearly screamed at him, but I covered my mouth as soon as the words came out. "I-I'm so sorry. I don't know why I said that."

"You're just upset, Amber. I get it. First, your boyfriend cheats on you, and now the one thing you want from me, you can't have."

"Why won't you just drink one? Even a couple sips?"

Ross' face fell, his shoulders slack. "It's not that I don't want to. It's that I can't. I've had alcohol before, Amber, and it does nothing but mess me up. I just don't wanna risk doing something I might regret, especially when I'm not inside my own home."

"Something you'd regret? Like what? You're the goodiest two-shoes I know!"

His face turned red as he blushed, his hands rubbing together like he was about to sweat bullets. "Something like kissing you."

I froze in place. "What?" *Had I heard that right?*

"Amber, I've liked you since I first met you, but since you were with Dawson, I couldn't do anything about it. So, I just friend-zoned myself, if that meant I could still hang out with you. But I hope you now understand why I can't take anything that'll screw up those inhibitions."

Hell, why was I still lying to myself? It wasn't like I hadn't felt the same way about Ross. We just seemed to fit better together than Dawson and I—whom I had absolutely nothing in common with. And he'd been there for me when all Dawson could do was ignore me and go behind my back with Cindy. What, are they dating now? Is it over between Dawson and I? Is that why he was *kissing* her?

I didn't give myself much time to think before I leaned over and pressed my face against Ross', taking him off-guard as he jumped back in surprise. I didn't want anything to stop me from doing what I was about to do.

"Whoa, whoa, Amber, hold up. You have a boyfriend." Ross shifted back in his seat and slowly inched away.

"Do I, though? Or is he out there cheating on me? And why are you against this? You literally just told me you liked me!"

"I do. I really do, but this doesn't feel right to me. You're in a vulnerable position, and I don't want to take advantage of you."

"But what if I told you I like you, too? More than I like Dawson."

"Amber, I don't know…"

But I leaned back in regardless, caressing his face against my hands and slowly moving my lips toward his. "Shh, don't say that. I want you, Ross, and I know you want me, too, so why are we fighting this?" I softly placed my lips over his and could taste the peppermint from his ChapStick, massaging first his upper lip, then his lower, with my own, and soon, I felt hands wrapping around my waist.

He leaned me back against the couch and continued to kiss me, wrapping me in his arms as if he were holding something precious that he didn't ever want to let go of. His kisses were gentle and meaningful, the complete opposite of Dawson's slobbery ones that always seemed to drench my face.

I reached behind him and slowly lifted his shirt while he continued to hold me dearly.

"Are you sure you want to do this?" he whispered into my ear, and when I nodded, he proceeded to take his shirt off for me. And his body, wow! It didn't look like Dawson's, with his muscular build and glaringly obvious tattoos, but Ross was jacked in his own right, and I definitely didn't mind the abs that were staring me in the face.

Then I felt his hands slide up my skirt cautiously, as it seemed he wanted to avoid whatever was going to sneak out and bite his fingers off. And as he did, he continued to kiss my chest, sliding the straps of my tank top off my shoulders and kissing lower and lower until…

My phone rang. I reached over to see who it was as Ross continued to plant kisses along the top of my breasts, his hands reaching higher and higher until I felt a shivering sensation shoot up my body.

It was Dawson. *What? Is he calling just to tell me how great Cindy's boobs are?*

I slapped the phone back down and let my thoughts wander through my brain. What was I doing? About to have sex with a guy I'd only just met? I lied there, still, for a moment while Ross continued to kiss me. The feelings of pleasure and revenge that I'd felt mere minutes ago were beginning to turn into guilt and regret, and I pushed Ross off of me.

"Why'd you do that?" he asked, clutching onto his left elbow. Must've fallen on his shoe or something.

"I-I'm sorry, Ross. I can't do this. You have to go."

"But I thought we were—"

"You have to go! Now!" I shouted and proceeded to throw his shoes out the door. Like a puppy who had just been kicked, he grabbed his shirt off the couch and walked out after them.

After I slammed the door behind him, I picked the unopened bottle of beer up off the table and threw it against the wall. The glass shattered, and the dark liquid oozed down the white paint, staining everything in its path as it dripped down to the floor. I screamed, louder than I'd ever screamed before, and I didn't care whether any of the neighbors heard.

I hated myself! I hated the life I was living! I'd been so optimistic about starting a new school in a new city, but this fucking town was full of nothing but fakes. Deceptive fakes who do nothing but use you and then screw you over.

"I hate you, Dawson!!"

Then my phone dinged. A text. I slowly dragged myself over to where I'd left my phone and picked it up.

Dawson.

DAWSON

Hey, can we talk?

I typed back.

AMBER

No.

DAWSON

Well, you don't really have much of a choice. I'm outside.

Chapter Seven

S hit! Did he see Ross? Did he see... us? I felt my body shaking aggressively as I stumbled over to the door. I peered through the side window of the front door, and there he was, waving at me. Now I *had* to open it.

I flung open the door, expecting Dawson to fume with anger, but he had his hands in his pockets and shuffled his feet on the door mat.

"Can I come in?" he asked.

I nodded and stepped off to the side. Everything felt so different now, so... awkward. The last time he'd been here, I leapt into his arms and made out with him on my bed. Now, I struggled just meeting him eye-to-eye.

"I saw Ross leaving your house."

Crap. He did see him. Did they talk? Does he know what I did?

"Well, what do you care? You fucked Cindy!" I didn't know why I was screaming. I hadn't meant to, but my frustration with everyone around me just sent me over the edge, and I didn't quite know how to dial it back.

"What the hell are you talking about?

"Cindy! It's all over school. You fucked her!" I yelled again.

"What?! Are you insane? No, I didn't!"

"But she said—"

"Amber! I don't care what she said. Who are you gonna believe? Your boyfriend, or someone who hates your guts enough to ruin it?" The look in Dawson's eyes were genuine, like he had nothing to hide.

"Then how do you explain her kissing you? By the lockers today?"

"You mean the kiss that she just threw on me? And if you'd watched a bit longer, you would've seen me pushing her away. Why are you interrogating me, anyway? You're the one who had another guy over."

"Wait, did you say you're still my boyfriend?"

"Yeah, were you fucking another dude?" The anger was starting to grow in his voice.

"So, does that mean Cindy made all that up? You never did anything with her?"

"Amber, if I did, wouldn't I be with her right now instead of standing here?" I stayed silent. "Are you gonna tell me what happened with Ross?"

"We're... we're just friends. That's all." I stuttered while trying to get those words out, and even I didn't believe what I had said.

"Bullshit, Amber. No guy wants to be just friends with a girl without wanting something more. Did you two fuck?"

"No! We didn't!"

"Then why was he here? At your house? In the middle of the fucking day?"

"Because I thought you were cheating on me, so I asked him to come over to cheer me up. But nothing happened, I swear!"

But he could tell that I was lying through my teeth. I was

never any good at lying, and it became glaringly obvious the more nervous I got.

"Oh, really? Then why do you have a dude's sock on your couch?"

I looked over to where he was nodding, and staring at me right in the face, was a black sock.

"Oh, that's just my dad's."

That was a mistake. Dawson walked over to where the sock was and picked it up. And to my demise, Ross' fucking mother had stitched his name on the inside tag!

"I'm sorry!" I blurted. "We just made out, but I swear, we didn't have sex! We were about to, but then you called, and I couldn't do it anymore. So, I kicked him out!"

"Why would you do that to me? How could you cheat on me? After everything we've been through?"

"Because I thought you were cheating on me! I'm so sorry, Dawson!" I clung onto his arm like plastic wrap. I didn't think I ever loved him, but the thought of losing him felt more terrifying that spending the rest of my life with him.

But he pushed me away. "I don't know, Amber. I trusted you. I love you, for fuck's sake! And you go ahead and pull this shit?"

"Please, Dawson, please don't go! Let me make this up to you! How can I get you to forgive me?"

"Kill Ross."

———

AND THAT'S how I found myself standing inside this warehouse. Dawson had given me an ultimatum—kill Ross, or lose him for good. The plan was to get him out of my life for good. Eliminate the threat. It was the only way Dawson could ever stay with me.

But I didn't know how to go through with it. The plan

was to lure Ross into the warehouse, giving him whatever he needed just to get him there, and then put a bullet through his head. But as the days counted down to that moment, I felt myself flickering back and forth between the two men in my life.

On the one hand, Dawson was hot, a god if I'd ever seen one. But we had nothing in common other than the fact that he'd taken my virginity. On the other hand, Ross was everything I'd ever wanted, a small-town boy with plenty to give and the promise of never betraying me.

But I loved Dawson. He was my first, and I wanted to give him what he wanted so we could stay together. Dawson. Ross. Dawson. Ross. Who do I choose? Or do I just walk away from them both?

"Amber, please! Don't do this! I beg you; don't do this!"

"Shut up! Shut up!" His voice sounded like nails down a chalkboard inside my ears, and if I'd had my second cup of coffee this morning, I may have just been a little more lenient. But I'm tired. I'm so tired of all the games, of all the lies, of the fucking ultimatum. "Just shut up, and let me think!"

The line between what I'd done to myself and what others had done to me was beginning to blur, and even though a part of me knew that none of this was exactly his fault, I couldn't find the strength to pull myself out of my trance.

I didn't plan for this to happen. Hell, I didn't even think I'd show up. Throwing on my pajamas and climbing into bed was my way of saying "no way in hell." I thought that if I slept through the night, I'd wake up the next morning scar-free.

But instead, somehow, I found my way here, holding a gun in my hand and aiming it at the man I once loved. Maybe because I knew that if I didn't take matters into my own hands, the two of them would end up dead the next day.

"Please, Amber. I'm sorry. For everything! You don't have to do this. I'll forgive you! Just please, don't pull the trigger."

His voice continued to stab against my brain, and every word felt like someone was ripping off a fucking nerve.

"I don't have to do this? I don't have to do this?! The nerve of you even saying that after what you've put me through, and now you have the audacity to ask me to stop?" I found myself yelling at him, my voice growing louder and louder by the second.

But in reality, I was just yelling at myself. At this little voice inside my head that refused to shut up. And if I'd recognized sooner that I was only taking my anger out on him, maybe this night wouldn't have ended in a bloodbath.

To be honest, I didn't even know why I'd been so angry. And if you asked, I couldn't pinpoint the exact moment when the words that came out of his mouth turned into a bullet straight through his head. But it did. And as I found myself trying to vigorously shake the anguish and stabbing pain out from my brain, I also found myself staring into my former lover's eyes, blood dripping from his mouth, followed by his body collapsing onto the ground and the shrieking scream of a female's voice.

Wait? Who else was here? I thought we were the only ones. Then who the *fuck* was yelling like a banshee that had just taken a knife to the heart?

Oh, right. Now I remember. It's *my* voice. *I* was the one screaming like a banshee.

I looked around me, and Ross was nowhere to be found. He must've snuck out the back when Dawson was begging for his life, and after a night of emotional terror, I found myself standing in front of a lifeless body, his blood pooling around my feet, with a smoking gun in my hand.

Isn't it funny how the moment you decide you want to continue living again is the same exact moment when it's gone forever? The universe has a funny way of showing its gratitude.

"I killed him," I whisper to the two older men standing in front of me, tears dripping onto the handcuffs that tightly wrap around my wrists. "I killed him!"

The metal bars slam shut as they thrust me inside a cold, dark cell, with nothing but a narrow bed and what resembled half a toilet bowl keeping me company. I turn around, screaming after the men as they begin to walk away.

"Wait! I... I can't stay here! I have to see him. I have to tell him I'm sorry!" I wrap my fingers around the metal bars, gripping with all the strength I could possibly muster, shaking it back and forth and screaming for the two men to come back.

"Should've thought of that before you shot him," one of them yells back from a distance, the echo bouncing off the walls.

Shot him. Yeah, I did that alright.

And now I'm facing life in prison.

A MONTH LATER, I receive a letter. It's from Ross.

Amber,

I still haven't forgotten about that night. I thought you were different. And I actually really liked you. But then everything that happened with Dawson, the lies, the manipulation. I mean, what were you thinking? Putting a bullet through a man's head? To someone you used to love?

Anyway, I just wanted to let you know that I still think about you from time to time, and

part of me wants to come see you, but I know
that'll just end badly for the both of us.
I've actually started seeing Cindy recently. For
a ditzy cheerleader, she's actually kind of
smart, and a great kisser. But I guess that's
the least of your concerns.
I hope things get better for you. As much as
they can, anyway.
Ross

I grip the crumpled sheet of paper in between my hands and can feel my entire body shake. *Cindy.* The bane of my fucking existence. She ruined my life since the first day I stepped into the godforsaken school, and I swear. I swear, if I ever get out of here, she's the first one I'm coming after.

The End

Stalk the Author

Website:
https://www.kathrynreign.com/

Facebook Page:
https://www.facebook.com/authorkathrynreign

Instagram:
https://www.instagram.com/authorkathrynreign/

Goodreads:
https://www.goodreads.com/author/show/21854875.
Kathryn_Reign

BookBub:
https://www.bookbub.com/authors/kathryn-reign

Murder in Miami

* 9 7 8 1 9 5 9 6 7 1 1 0 7 *